Dear Parents and Educators,

Welcome to Penguin Young Readers! As paren[t]
know that each child develops at his or her ow[n]
speech, critical thinking, and, of course, readi...
Readers recognizes this fact. As a result, each Penguin Young Readers
book is assigned a traditional easy-to-read level (1–4) as well as a
Guided Reading Level (A–P). Both of these systems will help you
choose the right book for your child. Please refer to the back of each
book for specific leveling information. Penguin Young Readers features
esteemed authors and illustrators, stories about favorite characters,
fascinating nonfiction, and more!

Kate & Mim-Mim: Little Kate Riding Hood

LEVEL **2**

GUIDED
READING
LEVEL **I**

This book is perfect for a **Progressing Reader** who:
- can figure out unknown words by using picture and context clues;
- can recognize beginning, middle, and ending sounds;
- can make and confirm predictions about what will happen in the text;
  and can distinguish between fiction and nonfiction.

Here are some **activities** you can do during and after reading this book:
- Compare/Contrast: In this story, Mim-Mim tells his own version of a
  classic fairy tale. Which parts of his story are the same as the original?
  Which parts are different?
- Sight Words: Sight words are frequently used words that readers
  must know just by looking at them. They are known instantly, on sight.
  Knowing these words helps children develop into efficient readers. As
  you read the story, have the child point out the sight words below.

again	could	her	just	once
ask	has	him	know	some

Remember, sharing the love of reading with a child is the best gift
you can give!

—Sarah Fabiny, Editorial Director
  Penguin Young Readers program

*Penguin Young Readers are leveled by independent reviewers applying the standards developed by Irene Fountas
and Gay Su Pinnell in *Matching Books to Readers: Using Leveled Books in Guided Reading*, Heinemann, 1999.

PENGUIN YOUNG READERS
An Imprint of Penguin Random House LLC

© 2016 KMM Productions Inc. a Nerd Corps company. Licensed by FremantleMedia Kids & Family
Entertainment. Based on the episode "Little Kate Riding Hood" written by Julie & Scott Stewart.
Published in 2017 by Penguin Young Readers, an imprint of Penguin Random House LLC,
345 Hudson Street, New York, New York 10014. Manufactured in China.

ISBN 9780515157710   10 9 8 7 6 5 4 3 2 1

Kate & Mim-Mim

Little Kate Riding Hood

by Lana Jacobs

Penguin Young Readers
An Imprint of Penguin Random House

Kate is in bed.

She cuddles Mim-Mim tight.

"What story would you like to

hear tonight?" asks Kate's mom.

"I know! How about Little Red

Riding Hood?" says Kate.

"One of my favorites!

Let me go find the book,"

says Kate's mom.

"What was it called again?

Little Pajama Pants?" she jokes.

"Mom is so silly, just like you,
Mim-Mim!" says Kate.
"I wonder what the story
would be like if you told it?"
she says.

That gives Kate an idea.

She twirls away with Mim-Mim.

Now they are in Mimiloo!

Kate and Mim-Mim see

their friends.

"Hooray! Mim-Mim is in

the story chair," says Lily.

"What kind of story
should I tell?" asks Mim-Mim.
"Little Red Riding Hood!"
says Lily.

Mim-Mim feels nervous.

He doesn't remember how to

tell the story.

"Just tell the story in your own way," says Kate.

Mim-Mim thinks for a moment.

"Once upon a time there was a girl named Little Kate Riding Hood," begins Mim-Mim.

Mim-Mim continues
telling the story.
Little Kate Riding Hood
has a job to do.
She has to bring a cake
to her Grand-Mim's house.
"What kind of cake was it?"
asks Lily.

"What kind of cake

should I choose?"

Mim-Mim asks Kate.

Kate tells Mim-Mim he can

choose any kind he likes.

That is the fun of telling stories!

Little Kate Riding Hood opens
her basket and sniffs.

"Carrot cake!" she exclaims.

She gives her mom a kiss
and skips down the road.

Little Kate Riding Hood

bumps into her friends

along the way.

"Hello, Gardener Gobble

and Woodsman Tack!" she says.

They warn Little Kate about

the big bad wolf.

But wait!

Mim-Mim does not want

there to be a wolf in his story.

"You could make him a swan!"

says Lily.

"Or a robot monkey," says Tack.

Mim-Mim has an idea!

"The Woodsman tells Little Kate
Riding Hood to watch out
for the Sneaky Lion,"
says Mim-Mim.
The Sneaky Lion wants to eat
Grand-Mim's cake!

The Sneaky Lion knocks on
Grand-Mim's door.

He has carrots for Grand-Mim.

Uh-oh!

The Sneaky Lion tricks

Grand-Mim.

He runs into Grand-Mim's house.

The Sneaky Lion dresses up
like Grand-Mim.

He will trick Little Kate
Riding Hood, too!

Little Kate Riding Hood knocks
on Grand-Mim's door.
She has some yummy carrot cake
for Grand-Mim.

"What big eyes you have,"
says Little Kate Riding Hood.
"The better to see you with,"
says the Sneaky Lion.

"What big teeth you have,"

says Little Kate Riding Hood.

"The better to eat cake with!"

says the Sneaky Lion.

The Sneaky Lion jumps at

Little Kate.

"Nobody tricks my Kate!"

Mim-Mim says.

He changes the story.

Everybody is excited now.

"What happens next?"

the friends ask.

Grand-Mim runs into the house.

She hears Little Kate Riding

Hood screaming for help.

Grand-Mim races to the rescue!

But the Sneaky Lion escapes.

Gardener Gobble and Tack the

Woodsman can help!

Mim-Mim uses his imagination

to finish the story.

"A Brave Bunny appears to save Little Kate and stop the Sneaky Lion!" says Mim-Mim.